NEW YEAR'S POEMS

SELECTED BY

MYRA COHN LIVINGSTON

ILLUSTRATED BY

MARGOT TOMES

HOLIDAY HOUSE/NEW YORK

For ANNA, LOUISE, JAY, and ROBERT, and
the happy new years ahead

M.C.L.

For BETTY MAIN

M.T.

Text copyright © 1987 by Myra Cohn Livingston
Illustrations copyright © 1987 by Margot Tomes
All rights reserved
Printed in the United States of America
First Edition

Library of Congress Cataloging-in-Publication Data

New Year's poems.

Summary: A collection of poems celebrating the New
Year by a variety of authors.
1. New Year—Juvenile poetry.   2. American poetry—
20th century.   3. Children's poetry, American.
4. Children's poetry, English.   [1. New Year—Poetry.
2. American poetry—Collections.   3. English poetry—
Collections]   I. Livingston, Myra Cohn.   II. Tomes,
Margot, ill.
PS595.N4N48   1987   811'.008'033   86-22885
ISBN 0-8234-0641-5

CONTENTS

JANUARY 1

FEBRUARY

6

JANUARY ONE

Said Jan to Feb:
"Came in on the ebb
Of the tide; saw Dec,
Poor soul, just cease
To be. 'Good-bye,'
He waved as I,
Unknown, was born
To the blare of horn,
Sound of whistles, bells,
Which are still what tells
Us the world has burned
Its bridges, turned
A page in Time;
Better yet, that I'm
The King of Now
For the moment. How
People act who made
Resolutions, prayed
For a change of pace;
Prayed the human race
Will improve its lot
In the new Year's what
Only Faith can bring
To pass. The thing
Has failed before—
Always as of yore.
Listen, Feb and Mar;
You'll know where we are
When your day comes," said Jan.
"Do your best. Back my plan
To plug Faith, to kill Fear.
Have a Happy New Year!"

DAVID McCORD

7

CHINESE NEW YEAR

Sugar and fruit for the Kitchen God
Whenever the New Year comes;
A new felt cap for old Papa
For old Mama, a cake of plums.

For the boys, some firecrackers,
For the girls, flowers bright and new,
But sugar and fruit for the Kitchen God
Whenever the New Year's due.

Adapted from *Chinese Mother Goose*

8

PROMISES

On New Year's Eve the snow came down
And covered every inch of town.
The next day winter sheets of white
Invited us to come and write
Our resolutions in the snow
So everyone in town would know
Of all the things we planned to do
To make the year completely new.

I dressed up warmly, then went out.
In single tracks I walked about,
Then found a spot ringed round with weeds
That seemed just perfect for my needs.
I took a breath and then jumped back
To keep a distance from my track,
And lay me down, my cheeks aglow,
To make an angel in the snow.

JANE YOLEN

RING OUT, WILD BELLS

Ring out, wild bells, to the wild sky,
    The flying clouds, the frosty light:
    The year is dying in the night;
Ring out, wild bells, and let him die.

Ring out the old, ring in the new,
    Ring happy bells, across the snow:
    The year is going, let him go;
Ring out the false, ring in the true . . .

ALFRED, LORD TENNYSON
From: *In Memoriam*, CVI

THE NEW YEAR'S JOURNEY

The New Year lives a long way off
When first it gives a little cough
And modestly but proudly glowing
Says: "Well, I guess I must be going."

Its solar engine starts to run
Ten billion years beyond the Sun
Out where the Universe begins
And ends—or turns around and spins.

Instantly it steps on the gas:
See? you can watch its needle pass
From zero to the speed of light
    In no time flat!
    How about that!
You'd never miss IT in the night.

And on it drives ten billion years.
Headed straight for our Earth it steers,
Its number shining on its back
Through all of Space's velvet black

Until its splashdown in the Pacific
(Along the Date Line to be specific)
Runs its banner round the world
Till the whole day has been unfurled.

It adds its tock to last year's tick:
You hear a click, you check your clock:
It's here! It's finally arrived!
Another New Year has survived

Its journey out of outer space.
That sleepy grin across its face
Says, "Well, I sure have stayed up late."
Now it proceeds at slower rate

To fill our lives with all the things
And people that a New Year brings
(You'll be amazed what it can hold!)
Before it gradually grows old.

But then you'll hear a long way off
The *next* New Year's brief, modest cough . . .

JOHN RIDLAND

THE BELL HILL

Out of the doors
our feet dash the red ground.
There is a sound

        like ringing
        as we touch down.

        It is New Year New Year
                New Year
All around

        We hear the voices
        of greeting cheer
        in the warm South.

On the radio
the weather forecaster
speaks of ice and snow.
On television
the children of the North
dress full cover and walk the glistening ice.
What a show!

It is New Year New Year
                        New Year
Far away and near
there is joy in the warm South.

Birds in the yellow sun sing and we sing
                        our voices ring
                        over Bell Hill
                        over the red clay:

It is New Year New Year
New Year
                        It is New Year's Day!

JULIA FIELDS

15

NEW YEAR'S ADVICE FROM MY CORNISH GRANDMOTHER

On New Year's Eve, at your front door
    Set out a silver pin
To fetch inside on New Year's morn
    That riches may flow in.

And in the new year, oh, don't dare
    (Lest all your luck be curst)
Let any person with red hair
    Step through your doorway first!

Let who is eldest first break fast
    And let the baby sleep.
Then dust away the old year's dust
    And kiss a chimney sweep.

X. J. KENNEDY

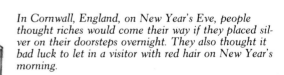

In Cornwall, England, on New Year's Eve, people thought riches would come their way if they placed silver on their doorsteps overnight. They also thought it bad luck to let in a visitor with red hair on New Year's morning.

16

17

FIRST JANUARY WALK

I've been out walking
among the winds of dawn.
I've kicked frozen puddles
and cracked them into crystal bits.
I've stepped on snow
and left my footprints
to melt in the afternoon sun.
I've run after deer
and felt no fear
of losing myself
in the open woods.
Pine trees have given me
their evergreen secrets,
and one or two blue jays
have sung to me.
I am free
with the New Year's air.

EMANUEL DI PASQUALE

18

NEW YEAR

After Christmas
The old
Year pales, its
Luxury stales, its
Garish wrappings
And trappings
Go out
Of style.

Time now
To start
Afresh, to
Throw away
The beautiful
Trash, to try
The antiseptic
Fashion of snow.

VALERIE WORTH

19

NEW YEAR'S EVE: OPELOUSAS, LOUISIANA

For Penny

Every one on Franklin Street
be up late,
popping popcorn on the stove,
sitting round to wait

for when the Old Year pack his things
and tell us folks good-bye;
big Roman candles sizzling up
to sparkle in the sky

and firecrackers shooting off,
while we right there to greet
a New Year fixing for to come
to live on Franklin Street.

MYRA COHN LIVINGSTON

21

FIRST FOOT

One . . . . two . . . . three . . . . four . . . .
Midnight knocking at our door.

A tall dark stranger waits outside
Turning away, his face to hide.

A lump of coal in one black hand—
What does it mean? Why does he stand

Holding his other hand out to us all
As we welcome him into the midnight hall?

Goodbye to the old year, good luck in the new,
"Come in, dear friend, peace be with you."

IAN SERRAILLIER

*In the coal-mining Black Country in England, there's
an old custom that a dark man "brings the New Year
in" by visiting his friends as the old year ends. The gift
of coal is to wish them "warm home, warm hearts."*

HERE SHE COMES!

Here she comes!
Burn the bonfire,
Bang the drum,
Hear the laughter spout and run
From her wide and happy mouth, now
Here she comes!

She comes dancing!
In the crackling yellow light
Her skirts swirl and fill the night,
Arms swaying,
Feet prancing,
She comes dancing!

Let's join her!
I feel fire in my skin,
As we all begin again
The ancient circling of the year;
Take her hand now, she draws near!
Happy New Year!

DEBORAH CHANDRA

OH CALENDAR!

To see
December press
Its face against the door,
I realize I've grown an inch
Or more

Since we
First hung you up.
You measured time by turns:
Hard winter nights to softball days,
Sunburns,

The chill
At Halloween,
Then! rumors of reindeer
Across the sky. Good-bye, Happy
Old Year!

J. Patrick Lewis

MIDNIGHT

After waiting up
Half the night
In tinselly hats
And noisy anticipation,

We open the door
to hear the New
Year sounding its
Whistles and bells

Through the dark,
Like a brilliant
Punctual train pulling
Into the station.

VALERIE WORTH

WATCHING THE NEW YEAR'S EVE PARTY
THROUGH THE STAIRCASE

Now midnight's here,
    The year is gone;
The merrymakers
    Carry on.

Instead of hats,
    They've sprouted horns
That make them look
    Like unicorns.

Tin whizzers buzz,
    Click-clackers clap,
Confetti snows
    Down Mrs. Knapp.

My Mother's fruitcakes
    Disappear.
The dancers shake
    The chandelier,

The floor, the windows . . . !
    Maybe this
Is why they stop
    Sometimes and kiss.

J. PATRICK LEWIS

THE YEAR
goes
skid-
ding
down
to
the
bot-
tom
of
the
cal-
en-
dar
slip-
ping
out   HAPPY NEW YEAR!
the   top.
end.   the
Then   to
Z O O M . . . . . . UP

FELICE HOLMAN

BEGINNING A NEW YEAR MEANS

taking off
 clothes spattered with
 chocolate milk
 and mud
throwing away
 scribbled pages
 full of crossed out words
 and mistakes
watching
 old snow
 melting away

putting on
 clean clothes
 without spots or wrinkles
opening
 white pages
 with nothing written
 on them yet
watching
 fresh snow
 falling
 without tiremarks
 or footprints

    RUTH WHITMAN

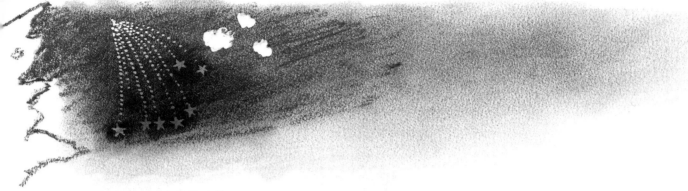

ACKNOWLEDGMENTS

Grateful acknowledgment is made to the following poets, whose work was especially commissioned for this book:

Deborah Chandra for "Here She Comes!" Copyright © 1987 by Deborah Chandra.

Emanuel di Pasquale for "First January Walk." Copyright © 1987 by Emanuel di Pasquale.

Julia Fields for "The Bell Hill." Copyright © 1987 by Julia Fields.

X. J. Kennedy for "New Year's Advice from My Cornish Grandmother." Copyright © 1987 by X. J. Kennedy.

J. Patrick Lewis for "Watching the New Year's Eve Party through the Staircase" and "Oh Calendar!" Copyright © 1987 by J. Patrick Lewis.

Myra Cohn Livingston for "New Year's Eve: Opelousas, Louisiana" and an adaptation of "Chinese New Year" from *Chinese Mother Goose Rhymes* by Isaac Taylor Headland, Fleming H. Revell Co., copyright 1900. Copyright © 1987 by Myra Cohn Livingston.

David McCord for "January One." Copyright © 1987 by David McCord.

John Ridland for "The New Year's Journey." Copyright © 1987 by John Ridland.

Ian Serraillier for "First Foot." Copyright © 1987 by Ian Serraillier.

Valerie Worth for "Midnight" and "New Year." Copyright © 1987 by Valerie Worth Bahlke.

Ruth Whitman for "Beginning a New Year Means." Copyright © 1987 by Ruth Whitman.

Jane Yolen for "Promises." Copyright © 1987 by Jane Yolen. Reprinted by permission of Curtis Brown, Ltd.

Grateful acknowledgment is also made for the following reprint:

Felice Holman for "The Year" from *The Song in My Head*. Copyright © 1985 by Felice Holman. Reprinted with the permission of Charles Scribner's Sons.